IMAGINE THAT

Licensed exclusively to Imagine That Publishing Ltd
Tide Mill Way, Woodbridge, Suffolk, IP12 1AP, UK
www.imaginethat.com
Copyright © 2023 Imagine That Group Ltd
All rights reserved
0 2 4 6 8 9 7 5 3 1
Manufactured in China

Written by Isabel Pope
Illustrated by Natalie Merheb

ISBN 978-1-80105-580-2

A catalogue record for this book is available from the British Library

Goodnight, Sleep Tight

Written by
Isabel Pope

Illustrated by
Natalie Merheb

Little one,
it's time for bed,

Time to rest your
sleepy head.

It's the end
of a fun day,

Let us plan tomorrow's play.

Now we are home,
safe and sound,

Where our cosy beds are found.

Let your worries fall away,

Soon there'll be a bright new day.

As the moon begins to gleam,

Snuggle up and start to dream.

While the stars shine like the sun,

Goodnight, sleep tight,
my little one.